Barbie™
and the
Scavenger Hunt

By Mary Packard

Illustrated by S. I. Artists

A GOLDEN BOOK • NEW YORK

Golden Books Publishing Company, Inc., Racine, Wisconsin 53404

"Girls, today is the last day of camp," Barbie said to the Trail Blazer Club one summer morning. "So I have something fun planned—a scavenger hunt!"

After breakfast the campers gathered in pairs around Barbie.

Barbie handed each pair a list.

"The first pair to find everything on this list wins," she said. "In an emergency, use our whistle code—three short toots and a long one. And don't leave your buddy. Okay?"

Within minutes Skipper and her friend Jen had
found an aluminum can and a bottle cap.
Skipper pointed toward the forest. "We'll find the
pine nut we need up there," she said.

Just then the girls heard their friends Tina and Rachel calling them.

"Come see what we've found," Tina shouted.

"Go ahead, Skipper," said Jen. "I'll wait."

"Look—a four-leaf clover!" said Tina.
"Too bad it's not on the list," added Rachel
"It will bring you good luck!" said Skipper.
"Maybe you'll win the scavenger hunt."

"How are you doing so far?" asked Tina.

Skipper opened her bag to show Tina and Rachel what she and Jen had found.

"I'd better get back to Jen now," said Skipper. "Hey, where is she? Jen!"

Jen didn't hear Skipper calling. She had gone
into the forest to find the pine nut they needed.
"Mmm, it smells good in here," she said. As she
reached down for a pinecone, a rabbit scampered by.

Jen ran to follow it. The rabbit bounded into some bushes and disappeared. Peering through the brush, Jen found an opening to a cave.

"I can't wait to tell everyone what I've found," she thought, as she crept in. Suddenly she slipped on a wet stone and fell down hard.

"Ow!" she cried. "My ankle! Somebody, help!"

"Help—help—help!" echoed her voice.

Jen pulled out her whistle, but it fell with a clatter into the darkness.

Meanwhile Skipper thought Jen might be hiding. "Okay, Jen," she called. "You win. I give up."

But when Jen still didn't appear, Skipper began to worry: "How could Jen just vanish?"

Skipper gave three short toots and a long
one on her whistle, hoping that someone would
hear her signal for help.

Skipper was glad to see Barbie and the Trail
Blazers running toward her a few minutes later.
"I can't find Jen anywhere," Skipper cried.
"You were right to call for help," said Barbie.

"Now, I'd like two Trail Blazers to stay here in case Jen walks by," she said, "and the others to come with Skipper and me."

The group walked farther into the forest. "Look!" said Barbie. "A barrette!"

Skipper quickly picked it up. "It's Jen's!" she said. Just then the Trail Blazers heard a faint "help!"

Barbie ran over to the brush. "Jen! We hear you
and we'll be right in!" she called. "Are you all right?"
"Yes, but I sprained my ankle," Jen called back.

"Barbie!" cried Jen. "Am I glad to see you!"
"We were so worried!" said Barbie.

"I was in such a hurry to win the scavenger hunt that I didn't wait for Skipper," explained Jen. "When I found this cave, I went in without thinking! Then I lost my whistle. I'm sorry."

"I'm just glad you're safe," said Barbie.

Skipper tore off part of her old T-shirt, and Barbie showed the girls how to wrap Jen's swollen ankle with it.

Later that night the girls gathered around the campfire.

"It's time for our scary story now," said Barbie with a wink. "Once upon a time, a girl went exploring all alone in a deep, dark cave. . . ."

"Uh, I think I'll go to bed early tonight!" said Jen.
"I won't need to hear any spooky stories for a long
time! Good night, everybody!"